This book belongs to:

. . . .

Contents

Peppa Meets The Queen

Peppa and her family are watching television.
Suddenly, there is a special announcement
from the Queen.

"The Queen! The Queen!" Peppa cheers.
"Hello to you all," the Queen says.
"Today, I have decided to give an award to the
hardest-working person in the country."

"The hardest-working person
in the country is . . .
Miss Rabbit!"

At the supermarket, Miss Rabbit
is closing the shop when
Mr Zebra, the postman, presents
her with a golden letter.

Miss Rabbit,

Please come to my
palace to get a medal
for all your hard work.
Bring friends.

All the best,
The Queen.

"I can't visit the Queen! I've got too much work to do!" Miss Rabbit panics.
"Don't worry!" Peppa says.
"The Queen has made it a holiday!"

It is the day Miss Rabbit
visits the Queen.
Peppa and her friends are going too.
"We're off to see the Queen!
We're off to see the Queen!
Eee-aye-addy-oh
We're off to see the Queen!"
"Here we are!" Miss Rabbit squeaks.

"Look at all the fancy stuff!
Woof!" Danny Dog says.
"Don't touch anything!"
Miss Rabbit warns.

"Where is the Queen?" Emily Elephant asks.
"Quee-een!" Suzy Sheep calls. "Where are you?"

In another fancy room, there is a lady
sitting on a throne, knitting.
"Hello!" Peppa says. "Have you seen the Queen today?"
"I AM the Queen!" the lady says.

"The children are very excited to meet you, Your Majesty," says Miss Rabbit.

"I'm excited to meet all of you!" the Queen says,
standing up. "And now for Miss Rabbit's medal!
This is the Queen's Award for Industry.
Keep up the good work!"

14

The Queen puts a shiny gold medal
over Miss Rabbit's head.
"Cheers for Miss Rabbit!" the Queen says. "Hip, hip!"
"Hooray!" shout the children.

Miss Rabbit and the children wear their boots
to go out into the palace gardens with the Queen.
"Do you play in your garden all the time,
Your Majesty?" Danny Dog asks.

"I don't have time for playing, no,"
answers the Queen.

She suddenly stops. "Oh, dear! A muddy puddle.
Never mind. We can walk round it."
"You can't walk round a muddy puddle!" Peppa says.

"You have to jump in it!"
Peppa shows the Queen
how to jump up and down
in the muddy puddle.

"I say! That does look fun," the Queen says.
"Here one goes then!"
"STOP!" shouts Peppa. Everyone gasps.
"If you jump in muddy puddles," Peppa says, "you must wear your boots, Your Majesty."

The Queen goes inside and comes back
with her boots on.

Everyone loves jumping up and down in muddy puddles, including the Queen!

Peppa Pig's Family Computer

Mummy Pig is working on the family computer. She is typing very fast. Mummy Pig has a lot of important work to do today.

Daddy Pig is in the kitchen
making soup for lunch.

"Daddy?" Peppa asks. "Can we go and watch
Mummy on the computer, please?"
"Yes, as long as you don't disturb her," Daddy Pig says.

"Mummy?" Peppa asks. "Can George and I sit on your lap and watch you work?"

"Yes, as long as you both sit quietly," Mummy Pig agrees.

About a minute later, Peppa asks, "Can we play the
Happy Mrs Chicken game on the computer?"

Mummy Pig says, "We can play Happy Mrs Chicken later. But now I have to work."

Another minute later, Peppa asks, "Mummy? Can we help you work?" Peppa taps away at the computer like Mummy Pig.

"No, Peppa!" Mummy says. "You mustn't touch the computer while I'm working."

"Yes, George," Peppa says in a bossy voice.
"You mustn't do this." Peppa taps away again
and the computer flashes.

"Peppa! Stop!"
Mummy Pig says.
"Sorry, Mummy," Peppa says.
"I was just showing George
what not to do."

"Daddy Pig!" Mummy calls. "Can you mend the computer while I finish the lunch?"
"Uh . . ." Daddy Pig says. "I'm not very good with these things."

"Hmmm . . ." Daddy Pig pushes a button.

"Mmmm . . ." Daddy Pig pushes another button.

"Maybe if I switch it off and switch it on again . . ."

41

Daddy Pig has mended the computer!
"Hooray, Daddy!" shouts Peppa.

She and George jump up and down.
"Yes," Daddy Pig smiles. "I am a bit of
an expert at these things."

"Daddy," Peppa asks. "Can we play that computer game, Happy Mrs Chicken? Mummy said we could play it later," Peppa says. "And now it's later!"

"Well," Daddy Pig thinks for a moment,
"OK then." Daddy Pig starts
the Happy Mrs Chicken game.

"Ho, ho, ho!" Daddy Pig laughs as Peppa
and George play Happy Mrs Chicken.
"Snort!" Mummy Pig says as she comes into the room.
"I see the computer is working again!"

Peppa Pig

Peppa Goes Camping

Today, Peppa and George
are very excited.
They are going on holiday!
Daddy Pig has a surprise.
Honk, honk!

"It's a camper van," grunts Daddy Pig.
"Wow!" gasp Peppa and George.

"We're going on holiday!" sings Peppa.

"We're going on holiday, in our camper van! Snort!"

"Hmmm," says Daddy Pig, looking at the map.

"Daddy Pig!" cries Mummy Pig. "Are we lost?"

"Well, er," begins Daddy Pig, "yes!"

Granddad Dog and Danny Dog arrive.
"Hello," calls out Peppa. "We're lost!"

"Lost?" asks Granddad Dog, confused.
"Is your satnav broken?"
Peppa, George, Mummy and Daddy Pig
don't know what satnav is.

"Satnav is a computer that helps you find your way," explains Granddad Dog. "Welcome to the car of the future," bleeps the satnav.

"Can you tell us where to go?" asks Peppa.

"Go straight," replies the satnav.

Daddy Pig thanks Granddad Dog
and the family continue on their way.
"We're going on holiday," sings Peppa.
"We're going on holiday, in our camper van!"
Suddenly, the camper van is low on oil.
But Daddy Pig can't find the engine!

Mummy Sheep and Suzy Sheep arrive in their car.
"Hello, Suzy," cries Peppa. "We've lost our engine!"

"Lost your engine?" replies Mummy Sheep.
"I don't know a thing about engines,"
says Mummy Sheep. "But I'll have a look."

"I'm probably wrong, but this looks like an engine,"
says Mummy Sheep, lifting the boot.
"Well spotted, Mummy Sheep,"
gasps Daddy Pig, pouring oil into the engine.
Glug, glug!
Daddy Pig thanks Mummy Sheep
and the family are off again!

"Are we nearly there yet?" asks Peppa, sighing.

"Just up the next hill," says the satnav.

"You have reached your destination," says the satnav when they get to the top of a steep hill.

"Hooray!" everyone cheers.

"Time for bed," says Mummy Pig.

Peppa and George put on their pyjamas.

"But where will we sleep?" asks Peppa.

"Mummy Pig and I will sleep on this bed,"

says Daddy Pig, pressing a button.

Whirrr!

"Ta-da! A lovely big bed appears in the room.

"And you two will sleep upstairs like

you always do," says Mummy Pig.

"Watch this," says Daddy Pig,

pressing another button.

Whirrr! Click . . .

Suddenly, the camper van's roof lifts up and
a bunk bed appears. Daddy Pig tucks
Peppa and George into bed.
"The camper van is just like our
little house!" says Peppa.

"Goodnight, everyone,"
says the satnav.
"Sleep well!"

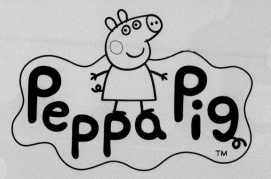

Peppa Plays Football

It's a sunny day and Peppa Pig and
Suzy Sheep are playing tennis.
"To you, Suzy!" cheers Peppa, hitting
the ball. Now it's Suzy's turn.
"To you, Peppa!" she cries, hitting the ball
straight over Peppa's head. Oh dear!

"Waaaa!" George feels a bit left out.
"Sorry, George," says Peppa. "You can't play
tennis. We only have two racquets."
"George can be the ball boy!" cheers Suzy.
"Being a ball boy is a very important job,
George," says Peppa.

Peppa and Suzy are having lots of fun,
but they keep missing the ball.
"Ball boy!" they shout together.
"Huff, puff!" George is not having fun.
He keeps running to get the ball and
he is very tired!

"Hello, everyone," cries Peppa when her friends arrive. "We're playing tennis." "Can we play too?" asks Danny Dog. "There aren't enough racquets," replies Suzy Sheep.

"Let's play football then,"
says Danny Dog.
"Football! Hooray!"
everyone cheers.

"We can play girls against boys," says Peppa.

"Each team needs a goalkeeper," says Danny Dog.

"Me, me!" shouts Pedro Pony.

"Me, me!" cries Rebecca Rabbit.

Pedro Pony and Rebecca Rabbit
decide to be the goalkeepers.
"The boys' team will start!" says Danny Dog.
Richard Rabbit gets the ball and runs
very fast, right by Peppa Pig,
Suzy Sheep and Candy Cat
and straight up to the . . .

. . . "GOAL!" cry Danny and Pedro together,
as Richard Rabbit kicks the ball straight
past Rebecca Rabbit and into the net.
"The boy is a winner!" cheers Danny Dog.
"That's not fair, we weren't ready," moans Peppa.

Rebecca Rabbit picks up the ball and runs.

"Hey!" shouts Danny Dog.

"That's cheating! You can't hold the ball."

"Yes I can!" says Rebecca. "I'm the goalkeeper."

Rebecca throws the ball into the goal,

straight past Pedro Pony.

"GOAL!" she cries.

"That goal is not allowed," says Pedro.

"Yes, it is," says Peppa.

"No, it isn't!" barks Danny.

"What a lot of noise," snorts Daddy Pig.

"I'll be the referee.

The next team to get a goal will win the game."

Richard Rabbit and George run off with the football, while everyone is still talking.

"Where's the ball?" asks Peppa.

But it's too late! Richard Rabbit kicks the ball straight into the goal, past Pedro Pony.

"Hooray! The boys win!" cries Danny.

"Football is a silly game," sighs Peppa, disappointed.
"Just a moment," says Daddy Pig. "The boys scored
in their own goal, that means the girls win!"
"Really?" gasp all the girls. "Hooray!"
"Football is a great game!" cheers Peppa.
"Ha, ha, ha!" everyone laughs.

Peppa Pig™

Fun at the Fair

Today, Peppa and her family are at the funfair.
"Snort! Slidey, slidey!" giggles George.
"George wants to go on the
helter-skelter," says Daddy Pig.
Daddy Pig and George head off to
the helter-skelter.

"Roll up! Roll up!" cries Miss Rabbit.

"Hook a duck and win a giant teddy!"

"I'll try to win one for you, Peppa," says Mummy Pig. "But I don't think it's that easy!"

"It's impossible!" laughs Miss Rabbit.

"We'll see about that!" cries Mummy Pig.

Sploosh! Mummy Pig has hooked a duck!

"Hooray!" cheers Peppa.

"That's amazing!" cries Miss Rabbit.

"Here's your giant teddy!"

"Wouldn't you like a little teddy instead, Peppa?"

"No way!" giggles Peppa, happily.

George and Daddy Pig are at the helter-skelter.

"Hmm, it's a bit high, George. Are you sure you want to have a go?" asks Daddy Pig.

George giggles and runs up the stairs to the top. It's a bit too high and George starts to cry.

"Don't worry, George. I'll come up with you," says Daddy Pig.

"Hee, hee! Weeeeeeee!" cries George,
sliding all the way down the helter-skelter.
Now, George is having too much fun to be scared.
"It is a bit high," says Daddy Pig nervously.
Daddy Pig is more scared than George.
Oops! Daddy Pig slips down the slide!

Wooahhh!

Peppa and Mummy Pig are at the
'Hit the Target' stall.

"You can do that easily, Mummy," says Peppa.

"Ho, ho! You won't win!" laughs Mr Labrador.

"Women are useless at this!"

"What did you say?" says Mummy Pig crossly.

She picks up the bow and arrow and aims . . .

Whoosh!

The arrow hits the target
right in the middle.

Mummy Pig wins again!

"Unbelievable," cries Mr Labrador. "Here's your teddy!"

"Hooray!" cheers Peppa.

Now she has **two** giant teddies.

Daddy Pig and George are
riding on the big wheel. George loves it,
but Daddy Pig is a little bit scared.
"This really is high!" says Daddy Pig, as the
big wheel goes round and round.
"Hee, hee! Snort!" giggles George.

Daddy Pig and George find Peppa and Mummy Pig.
"Hit this button with a hammer," says
Mr Bull. "If the bell rings, you win a prize!"
"I'll have a go," says Daddy Pig. "Stand back!"
"I think you're a bit wobbly from the big wheel!"
says Mummy Pig.

"Ho, ho!" laughs Mr Bull.
"Daddy Pig is looking a bit shaky!"

"What?" says Mummy Pig, crossly.
"Give . . . me . . . that . . . hammer!"
Whack! Mummy Pig hits the button
as hard as she can.
The bell rings loudly. Ding! Ding! Ding!

Everyone is very impressed. Mummy Pig wins
all the giant teddies at the fair!

"Hooray!" cheers Peppa and she gives all of
her friends one giant teddy bear each.
"Hooray!" everyone cheers. "We love funfairs!"

Peppa's First Sleepover

Peppa is going to her very first sleepover at Zoe
Zebra's house. "Welcome to my sleepover!" Zoe says.

"I'll pick you up in the morning," Mummy Pig
says to Peppa with a kiss.

Rebecca Rabbit, Suzy Sheep and
Emily Elephant are already here.
"I've got my teddy," Peppa says.

Zoe has her monkey. Rebecca has her carrot.
Suzy has her owl. And Emily has her frog.

125

"Don't stay up too late, girls! And don't be too loud.
Daddy Zebra has to get up early to deliver the post,"
Mummy Zebra says as she turns out the lights.

Zoe's baby twin sisters, Zuzu and Zaza,
want to join the sleepover too.
"Sleepovers are only for big girls!" Zoe says.

The twins begin to cry.
"They're so sweet and little," Peppa says.

"Can they stay?" Rebecca asks.
"OK," Zoe says to the twins.
"But you must NOT fall asleep."

"What should we do first?"
Suzy asks.
"I'm having piano lessons!
Listen . . ." Zoe starts to pound
on the keys. "Twinkle, twinkle,
little star . . ."

Mummy Zebra has woken up,
"Shush! You must be quiet so Daddy Zebra can sleep!
Now, into your sleeping bags, please."

"Snort! What do we do now?" Peppa asks. "At sleepovers, there's always a midnight feast!" Zoe says. "It's when we eat things," Suzy says in a hushed voice. "In secret."

"Shhh!" Zoe says as she leads the girls to the kitchen. They each grab some delicious fruit, perfect for a midnight feast. The floorboard creaks.

Oh no! Mummy Zebra has woken up. "You'll wake Daddy Zebra! Now, who knows a bedtime story?"

The girls take turns: "Once upon a time, there was a little fairy . . ." Suzy begins.

138

"And she lived in the forest . . ." Peppa continues. "And the fairy met a big monster, who went . . . RAARRR!" Emily says with a big elephant trumpet noise!

Oh dear. The noise has woken Daddy Zebra!
"Sorry, Daddy," Zoe says. "There was a story
about a fairy and a scary monster."

"And we want to know what happens next!"
Peppa says. "Very well," Daddy Zebra sighs.
"The monster lifted up his great,
big hairy paws . . ."

"And walked along on his great, big hairy feet . . . And sang . . . 'Twinkle, twinkle, little star, how I wonder what you are . . .'" Daddy Zebra sings gently as he plays the piano.

Daddy Zebra's song has
sent everyone to sleep.

143

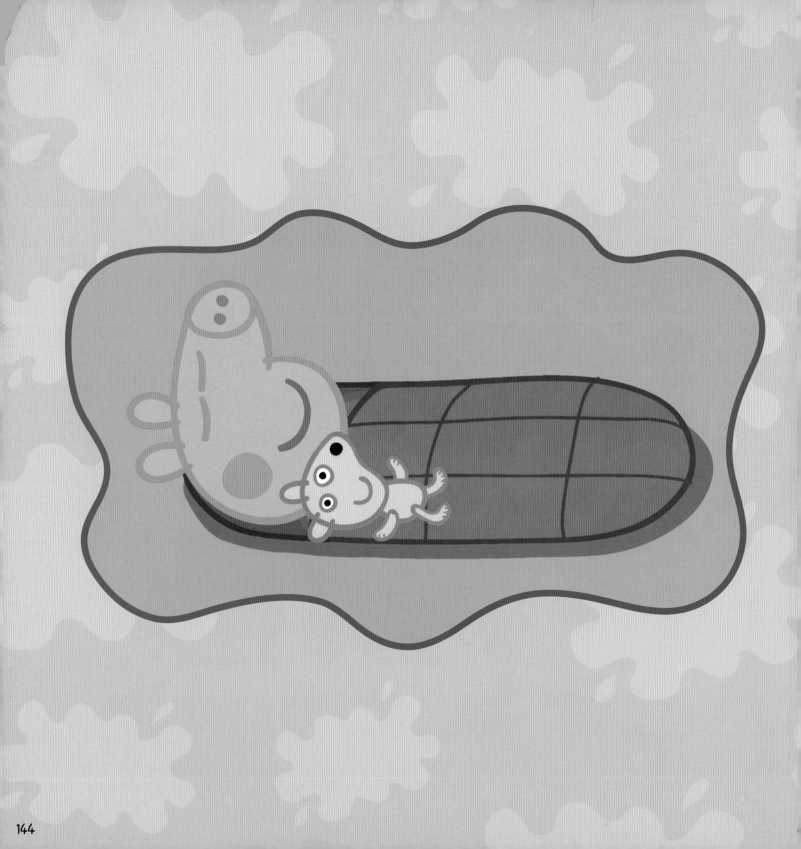